There's no escaping growing up, it's something we all do.

Each stage of life is different – exciting, fresh and new...

A newborn is a precious gift,
wrapped up in love and joy,
a cherished treasure to behold –
a brand new girl or boy.

Innocent and helpless, so perfect and complete,
as fragile as spun sugar and every bit as sweet!

Looking wide-eyed at the world, babies take in everything –
the sun's warm rays, the rustling leaves, the squeaking of a swing.

They stretch to feed the hungry ducks, with food clutched in their hands –
with each and every passing day, their tiny world expands.

Walking on unsteady legs, the toddler's on the move,
confidently striding out with everything to prove!

The world is now a playground – there's lots to touch and see!
For now they are adventurers who waddle off with glee.

In the country meadow, where the grasses swoosh and sway,
there's a free and headstrong spirit – a child who wants to play.

They use imagination to chase dreams through magic lands,
inventing words and language only they can understand.

Behind the library bookshelves sits a curious little mind –
there are many truths and answers that they have yet to find.

A student of the world,
asking "how?" and "what?" and "why?",
firing questions into space,
like rockets to the sky.

Stranded on an island
is a wild and restless teen –
unsure of their direction or
what their future means.

They grow into an adult, a journey wonderful and strange –
on a path to self-discovery, a confusing time of change.

Young adults sail
untethered ships
out into the sea.
They chart the course
that leads them
to who they're meant to be.

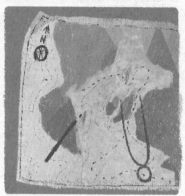

They battle whirlpools,
storms and tides
in their own lifeboat.
By riding peaks and
braving troughs,
they learn to stay afloat.

In the tangled woods of time,
the adult is a tree.
They put down roots to settle
and mature for all to see.

Some may live in luscious groves,
some live alone in style.
Adapting to life's challenges,
they're strong, yet versatile.

Sitting on the soft white sand, in a wistful state,

a person calmed by inner peace has come to meditate.

They pause, serene and confident, knowing who they are.
They have wisdom from life's lessons, for they have travelled far.

As the hillside glitters in the setting of the sun,
a wise and wrinkled watcher surveys everything they've done.

The earth beneath has shifted, a lifetime has passed by –
there's a comfort in the air as the sun sinks in the sky.

We are all astonishing – we grow in different ways
and the chapters of our lives create a story to amaze!

No one knows what lies ahead or what we'll grow to be,
it's all a part of growing up – the journey to be "me".